iR

CREATED FOR INTERNATIONAL RESCUE BY SIMON AND SCHUSTER
First published in Great Britain in 2015 by Simon and Schuster UK Ltd
1st Floor, 222 Gray's Inn Road, London WC1X 8HB
A CBS Company

ISBN 978-1-4711-2499-0
Printed and bound in China
10 9 8 7 6 5 4 3 2 1
simonandschuster.co.uk

THUNDERBIRDS

ARE GO

TB

OFFICIAL GUIDE

SIMON & SCHUSTER

WHEN DISASTER STRIKES
AND THERE'S NO ONE ELSE TO HELP,
INTERNATIONAL RESCUE
ANSWERS THE CALL!

From their hidden island base, the five Tracy Brothers pilot remarkable, cutting-edge Thunderbird craft to the depths of the oceans and to the limits of space – all for one reason: to help others in need.
Now you can join them; record your details here:

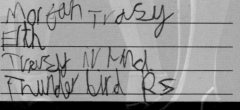

IR RECRUIT DETAILS:

» NAME: Morgan Tracy
» MISSION: Earth
» LOCATION: Tracy Island
» CRAFT: Thunderbird R5

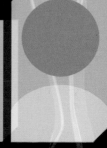

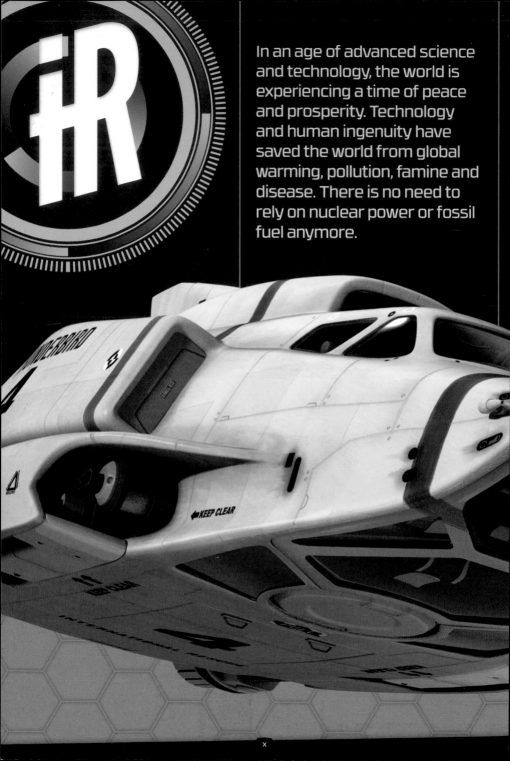

In an age of advanced science and technology, the world is experiencing a time of peace and prosperity. Technology and human ingenuity have saved the world from global warming, pollution, famine and disease. There is no need to rely on nuclear power or fossil fuel anymore.

This does not mean that the world is without problems - natural and manmade disasters still occur, accidents still happen and agents of evil are always at work to disrupt the peace. To combat this, an anonymous team was formed, for one reason alone - as a means of rescue when all other methods have failed. This organisation is **INTERNATIONAL RESCUE**.

Be it land, sea, air or space, nowhere is out of their reach. If no one can help someone in danger, **INTERNATIONAL RESCUE** will always answer the call.

INTERNATIONAL RESCUE identities are not widely known but their exploits are legendary. From their secret island base, the world knows them as a team of rapid responders who have expertly handled countless dangerous situations.

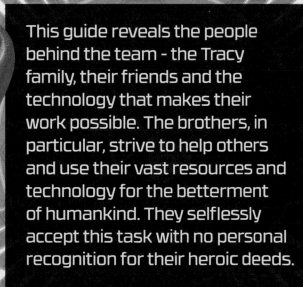

This guide reveals the people behind the team - the Tracy family, their friends and the technology that makes their work possible. The brothers, in particular, strive to help others and use their vast resources and technology for the betterment of humankind. They selflessly accept this task with no personal recognition for their heroic deeds.

CONTENTS

JOHN TRACY

- » **CRAFT:** THUNDERBIRD 5
- » **TASK:** SPACE COMMAND –
  COMMUNICATIONS
  AND DISPATCH
- » **LIKELY** "INTERNATIONAL RESCUE,
  TO SAY: WE HAVE A SITUATION"

THUNDERBIRD 5

THUNDERBIRD 5

INTERNATIONAL RESCUE

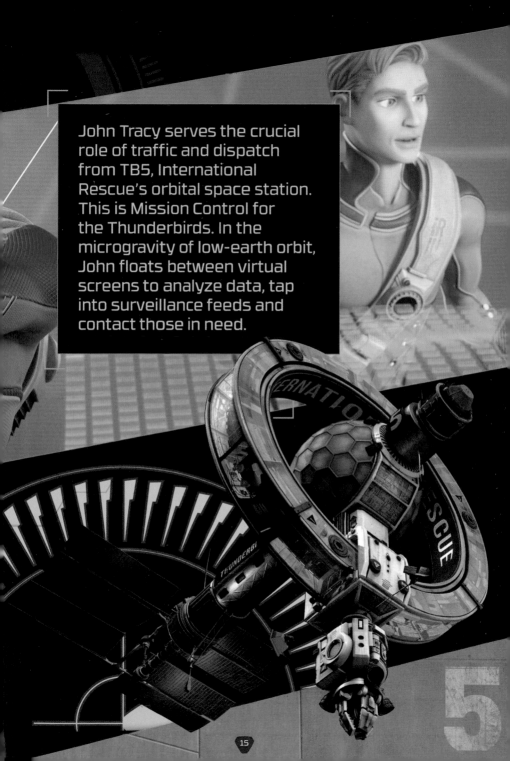

John Tracy serves the crucial role of traffic and dispatch from TB5, International Rescue's orbital space station. This is Mission Control for the Thunderbirds. In the microgravity of low-earth orbit, John floats between virtual screens to analyze data, tap into surveillance feeds and contact those in need.

As well as the many virtual screens in TB5, John also uses the holoprojector on his suit. With this, he can analyse data, tap into surveillance feeds and contact those in need. He thrives on the constant activity of monitoring every frequency on earth. He is very focussed on his role, almost to the point of obsession.

John can travel back to Tracy Island using a space elevator that seamlessly connects to TB5. However, he rarely uses this as he loves his role in space and knows how important it is for International Rescue.

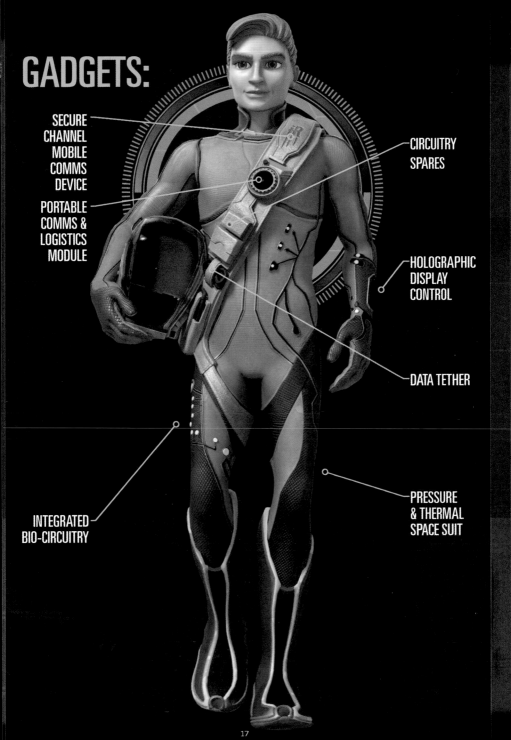

GADGETS:

SECURE CHANNEL MOBILE COMMS DEVICE

PORTABLE COMMS & LOGISTICS MODULE

CIRCUITRY SPARES

HOLOGRAPHIC DISPLAY CONTROL

DATA TETHER

INTEGRATED BIO-CIRCUITRY

PRESSURE & THERMAL SPACE SUIT

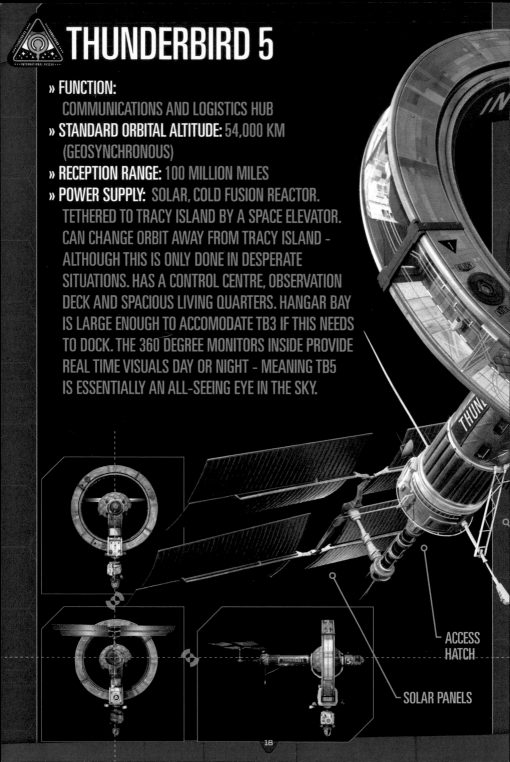

THUNDERBIRD 5

- » **FUNCTION:**
  COMMUNICATIONS AND LOGISTICS HUB
- » **STANDARD ORBITAL ALTITUDE:** 54,000 KM
  (GEOSYNCHRONOUS)
- » **RECEPTION RANGE:** 100 MILLION MILES
- » **POWER SUPPLY:** SOLAR, COLD FUSION REACTOR.
  TETHERED TO TRACY ISLAND BY A SPACE ELEVATOR.
  CAN CHANGE ORBIT AWAY FROM TRACY ISLAND –
  ALTHOUGH THIS IS ONLY DONE IN DESPERATE
  SITUATIONS. HAS A CONTROL CENTRE, OBSERVATION
  DECK AND SPACIOUS LIVING QUARTERS. HANGAR BAY
  IS LARGE ENOUGH TO ACCOMODATE TB3 IF THIS NEEDS
  TO DOCK. THE 360 DEGREE MONITORS INSIDE PROVIDE
  REAL TIME VISUALS DAY OR NIGHT – MEANING TB5
  IS ESSENTIALLY AN ALL-SEEING EYE IN THE SKY.

ACCESS
HATCH

SOLAR PANELS

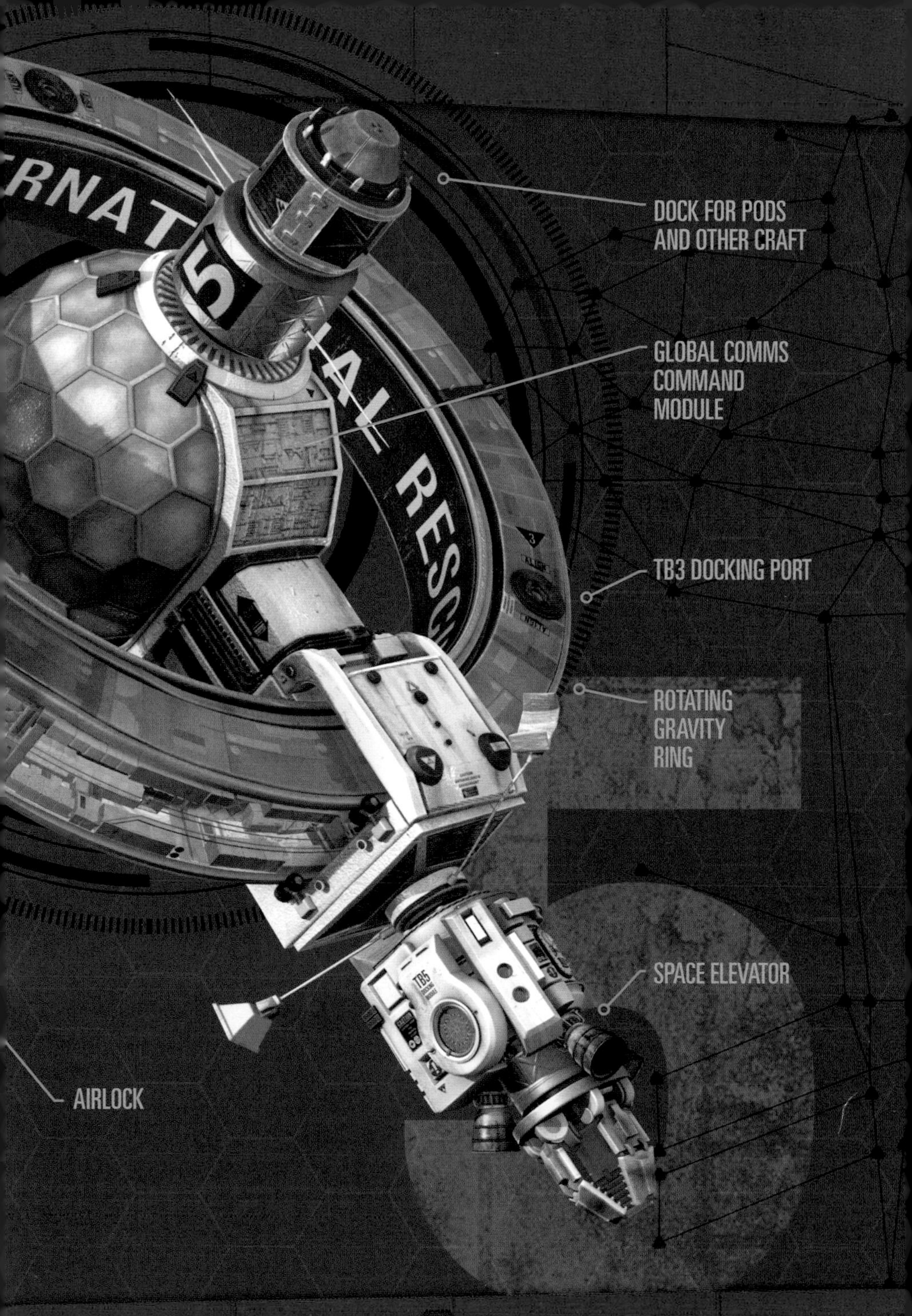

DOCK FOR PODS
AND OTHER CRAFT

GLOBAL COMMS
COMMAND
MODULE

TB3 DOCKING PORT

ROTATING
GRAVITY
RING

SPACE ELEVATOR

AIRLOCK

JOHN TRACY
// KEY MISSION REPORT:
EOS

» **LOCATION:**
  THUNDERBIRD 5'S GEOSTATIONARY ORBIT
  ABOVE TRACY ISLAND

» **OBJECTIVE:** A TYPICAL DAY FOR JOHN – MONITORING GLOBAL
  ACTIVITY

» **CRISIS:** THE ROGUE ARTIFICIAL INTELLIGENCE PROGRAMME
  KNOWN AS EOS GAINED CONTROL OF TB5. IT, IMPERSONATING
  JOHN, SENT FALSE MONITOR IMAGES TO TRACY ISLAND TO
  AVOID SUSPICION FROM THE OTHER BROTHERS

» **BREAKTHROUGH:** JOHN CONTACTED LADY PENELOPE OUTSIDE
  OF TB5 COMMS AND INFORMED HER OF THE SITUATION. ALAN
  RESCUED JOHN USING THUNDERBIRD 3

» **RESOLUTION:** JOHN PROVED THAT HE HAS THE A.I.'S BEST
  INTEREST IN MIND. JOHN AND EOS ASSUME CO-CONTROL
  OF THE STATION, WHICH NOW RUNS MORE EFFECTIVELY
  THAN EVER

» **LEARNING:** WORKING TOGETHER IS ALWAYS THE MOST
  EFFECTIVE WAY

GORDON TRACY

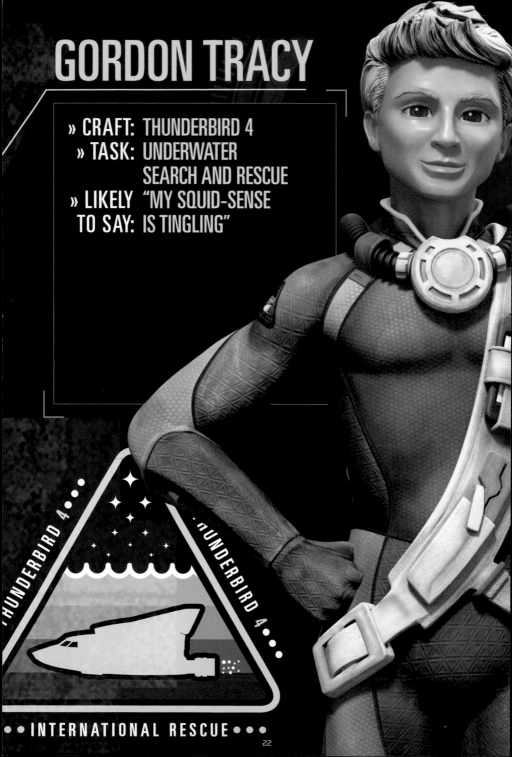

- » **CRAFT:** THUNDERBIRD 4
- » **TASK:** UNDERWATER SEARCH AND RESCUE
- » **LIKELY TO SAY:** "MY SQUID-SENSE IS TINGLING"

Pilot of the submersible Thunderbird 4, Gordon's domain is under the water. When he's not patrolling the depths of the oceans, TB4 is docked within TB2, meaning that Gordon is also occasionally Virgil's co-pilot. Gordon loves to joke around and be the comedian of the family. He has made it his life's ambition to make Virgil laugh and spends much of his time trying to come up with wisecracks – although they generally produce more groans than laughs.

THUNDERBIRD 4

KEEP CLEAR➡

PROFILE:

» GREAT SENSE OF HUMOUR, LOVES TO HAVE FUN
» LIVES LIFE TO THE FULLEST BUT SERIOUS WHEN IT COMES TO WORK
» OFTEN THE LOUDEST VOICE (AND SHIRT) IN THE ROOM
» SPECIALISED EQUIPMENT: TURBO-VORTEX PROPULSION DEVICE (AKA "AQUA SCOOTER")

Gordon wears a heavy-duty breathing regulator around his neck so he can breathe underwater, as well as in potentially harmful atmospheric conditions. He always travels with a motorised propulsion device which helps him make his way through water even more quickly. This also means he can squeeze through small spaces that TB4 would not be able to reach.

Although his vehicle and suit are mainly designed for working underwater, Gordon will happily take part in any rescue that needs him.

GADGETS:

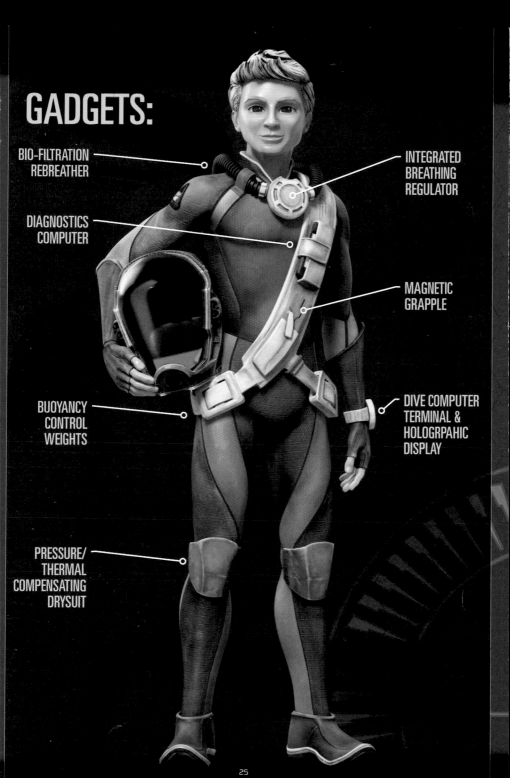

BIO-FILTRATION
REBREATHER

INTEGRATED
BREATHING
REGULATOR

DIAGNOSTICS
COMPUTER

MAGNETIC
GRAPPLE

BUOYANCY
CONTROL
WEIGHTS

DIVE COMPUTER
TERMINAL &
HOLOGRPAHIC
DISPLAY

PRESSURE/
THERMAL
COMPENSATING
DRYSUIT

THUNDERBIRD 4

- » **FUNCTION:** UNDERWATER SEARCH & RESCUE
- » **UNDERWATER SPEED:** 160 KNOTS
- » **EQUIPMENT:** ACTIVE 4D SONAR ARRAY, ADAPTIVE UTILITY ARMS, DEMOLITION TORPEDOES, QUICK-LAUNCH ESCAPE TUBES. HOVER JETS ALLOW IT TO TRAVEL SHORT DISTANCES OVER LAND. HIGHLY MANOEUVERABLE AND LIGHTNING QUICK IN THE WATER. REINFORCED HULL AND CABIN PRESSURISATION SYSTEM MEAN IT CAN REACH UNFATHOMABLE DEPTHS. CUTTING AND GRAPPLING ARMS BECOME A MECH-EXTENSION OF GORDON'S MOTION. ALSO HAS AN EXTENDABLE AIRLOCK THAT CAN BE USED TO ATTACH TO SUNKEN STRUCTURES.

ENGINE INTAKE

COCKPIT

SCANNING ARRAY

KEEP CLEA

THUNDERBIRD **4**

THUNDERBIRD **4**

HIGH
POWERED
LIGHTING

HATCH

684 987

DRY TUBES

DIVE JET

ROBOTIC EXTENSION ARMS AND HARPOON LAUNCHER

GORDON TRACY
// KEY MISSION REPORT:
RING OF FIRE
/SEA TRENCH RESCUE

» **LOCATION:**
UNDERWATER RESEARCH CENTRE

» **OBJECTIVE:** RESCUE THE SCIENTISTS ABOARD THE
DEEP-SEA RESEARCH CENTRE

» **CRISIS:** A SERIES OF GLOBAL UNDERWATER EARTHQUAKES HAVE
DESTABILISED THE OCEAN FLOOR MEANING THE RESEARCH
CENTRE IS UNSAFE AND THE ESCAPE HATCH IS BLOCKED

» **BREAKTHROUGH:** THUNDERBIRDS 1 AND 2 MANAGE TO
STABILISE THE CENTRE FROM ABOVE USING MAGNETIC
GRAPPLING CABLES BUT THUNDERBIRD 4 IS TRAPPED
IN A CAVE DURING ANOTHER SEAQUAKE

» **RESOLUTION:** TB4 ESCAPES THE CAVE AND FURTHER
AFTERSHOCKS AND RESCUES ALL MEMBERS OF THE RESEARCH
TEAM SENDING THEM TO THE SURFACE IN DRY TUBES

» **LEARNING:**
EVERY TEAM MEMBER ADDS VALUE TO A MISSION

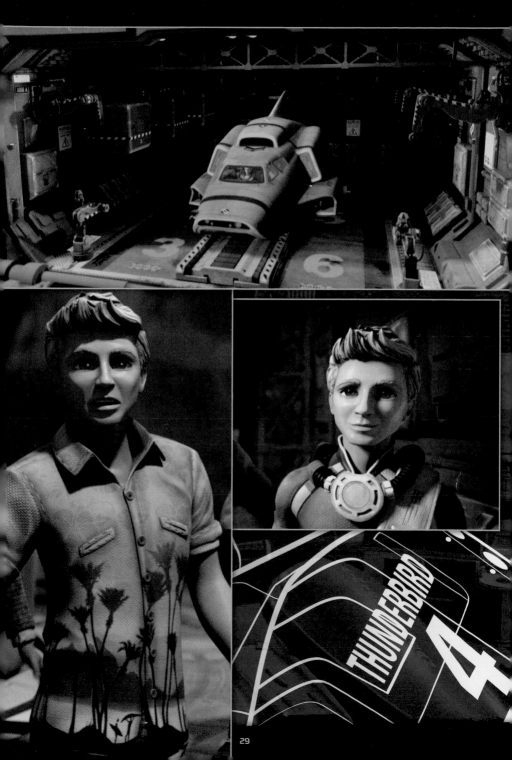

TRACY ISLAND

International Rescue has created a permanent base of operation on a remote island. To most observers Tracy Island looks nothing more interesting than an island in the middle of the ocean. Its secrets are safe from prying eyes. Hidden on the island are some of the most exciting and advanced technologies, equipment and vehicles in existence.

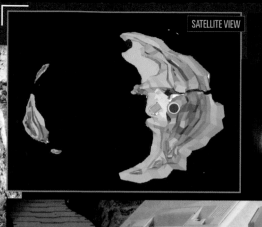

SATELLITE VIEW

TB-1 DELIVERY

ROBOTIC ARM IN USE

THUNDERBIRD 1 AND THUNDERBIRD 2 REFUELLING HANGAR

COMMS ROOM

Built on an extinct volcano, the island possesses enormous lava tubes and underground cave systems that provide a natural infrastructure for International Rescue. Cutting-edge technology is in use throughout the island including a team of autonomous maintenance robots.

KITCHEN

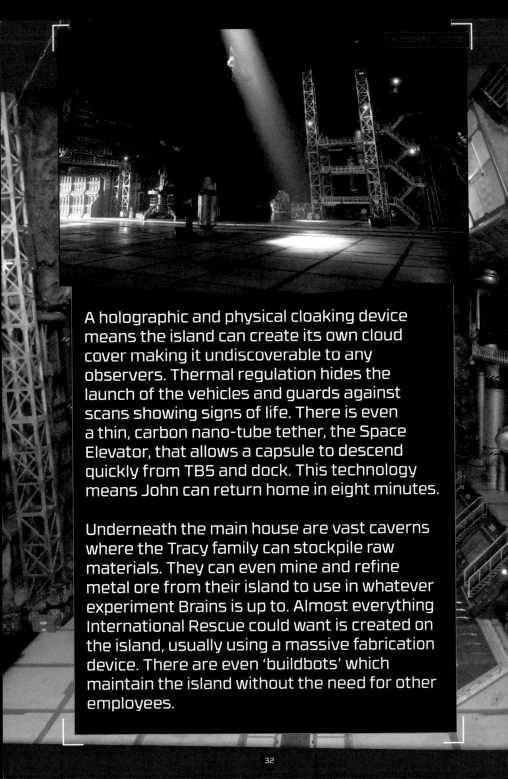

A holographic and physical cloaking device means the island can create its own cloud cover making it undiscoverable to any observers. Thermal regulation hides the launch of the vehicles and guards against scans showing signs of life. There is even a thin, carbon nano-tube tether, the Space Elevator, that allows a capsule to descend quickly from TB5 and dock. This technology means John can return home in eight minutes.

Underneath the main house are vast caverns where the Tracy family can stockpile raw materials. They can even mine and refine metal ore from their island to use in whatever experiment Brains is up to. Almost everything International Rescue could want is created on the island, usually using a massive fabrication device. There are even 'buildbots' which maintain the island without the need for other employees.

HANGAR AND TUNNEL LOCATION

THUNDERBIRD 4 LAUNCH

Four of the Thunderbird craft are docked on Tracy Island. Each of the brothers can reach their vehicles using an individual launch sequence route which starts in the living room. These transport tubes cross the island and mean the family can move from place to place within seconds — especially important if there is an emergency (or if a quick escape is needed from some of Grandma Tracy's cooking!)

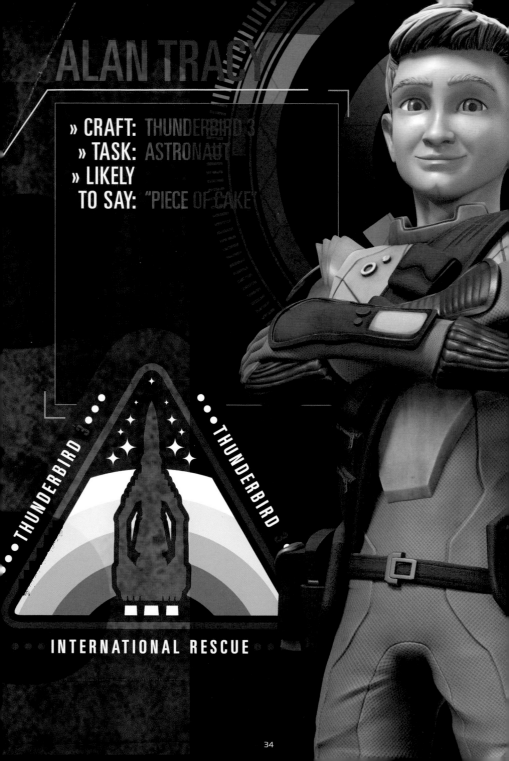

ALAN TRACY

» **CRAFT:** THUNDERBIRD 3
» **TASK:** ASTRONAUT
» **LIKELY
TO SAY:** "PIECE OF CAKE"

THUNDERBIRD 3

THUNDERBIRD

INTERNATIONAL RESCUE

Alan is pilot of Thunderbird 3 - International Rescue's orbital rocket ship. This is an amazingly complex machine to operate and manoeuvre — especially in space. Alan does so without breaking a sweat. He has almost superhuman reflexes and makes his rescues look almost effortless. People underestimate his talent at their own risk.

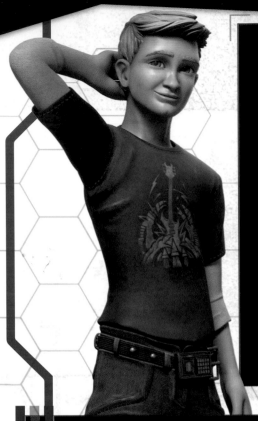

PROFILE:

» YOUNGEST, BUT MOST NATURALLY GIFTED PILOT
» ALMOST SUPERHUMAN REFLEXES AND INTENSE FOCUS
» ENTHUSIASTIC
» TYPICAL TEENAGER: LOVES SLEEP ALMOST AS MUCH AS HE LOVES HELPING PEOPLE

Thunderbird 3 doesn't get as much flight time as the other Thunderbird craft. This would bother any other Tracy, but not Alan. He loves playing video games, watching old kung fu movies and poking around Brains' lab. Brains appreciates Alan's contagious enthusiasm even if sometimes he wishes he didn't press buttons on his experiments or constantly ask questions.

Alan's main activity on the island is avoiding Grandma Tracy. He is always working hard to hide from her so she can't make him clean or taste test her latest cooking attempt!

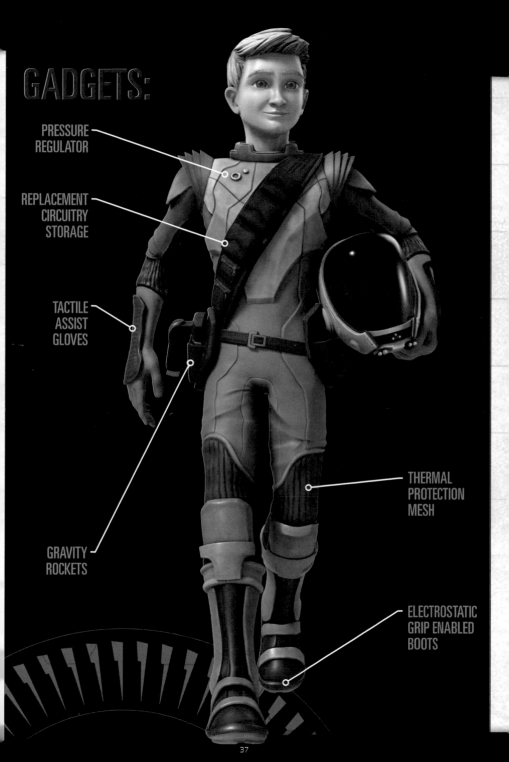

GADGETS:

PRESSURE REGULATOR

REPLACEMENT CIRCUITRY STORAGE

TACTILE ASSIST GLOVES

GRAVITY ROCKETS

THERMAL PROTECTION MESH

ELECTROSTATIC GRIP ENABLED BOOTS

THUNDERBIRD 3

» **FUNCTION:** SPACE RESCUE
» **LAUNCH SYSTEM:** HYBRID ELECTROMAGNETIC/ROCKET MOTOR
» **DRIVE SYSTEM:** ION-DRIVE PARTICLE ACCELERATOR
» **MAX ACCELERATION:** 10 G

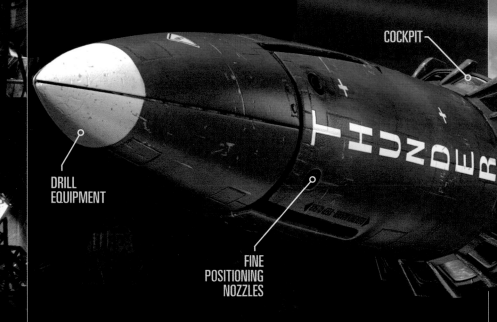

COCKPIT

DRILL
EQUIPMENT

FINE
POSITIONING
NOZZLES

» **EQUIPMENT:**
TRI-GRAPPLE GRASPING ARMS, INTERCHANGEABLE CARGO
SECTION, HIGHLY ADVANCED HEAT AND RADIATION SHIELDING.
DOES NOT USE COMBUSTIBLE PROPELLANT MEANING THAT IT
DOES NOT NEED TO CARRY HUGE AMOUNTS OF FUEL. COCKPIT
IS FIXED ON RAILS SO ALWAYS STAYS IN THE SAME POSITION
WHICHEVER WAY THE ROCKET ROTATES.

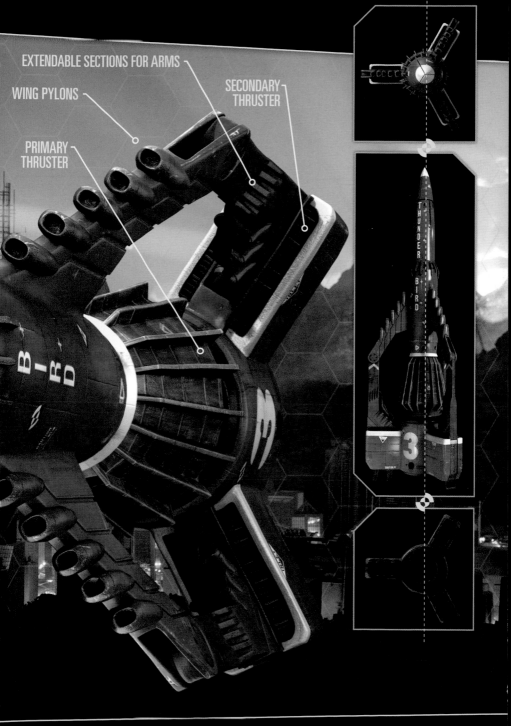

EXTENDABLE SECTIONS FOR ARMS

WING PYLONS

SECONDARY THRUSTER

PRIMARY THRUSTER

ALAN TRACY
// KEY MISSION REPORT:
SPACE RACE

» **LOCATION:**
   EARTH'S ORBIT

» **OBJECTIVE:** ALAN IS CLEARING DEBRIS FROM SPACE WHEN A DANGEROUS OLD ORBITAL MINE IS ACTIVATED

» **CRISIS:** THE MINE LOCKS ONTO THUNDERBIRD 3'S HEAT SIGNAL. ALAN MUST SAFELY DETONATE IT BUT HE NEEDS TO READ THE IDENTIFICATION NUMBER ON THE MINE FOR INTERNATIONAL RESCUE TO FIND THE RIGHT DEACTIVATION CODE

» **BREAKTHROUGH:** LADY PENELOPE AND PARKER MANAGE TO BYPASS SECURITY AT THE FACILITY WHERE THE DEACTIVATION CODE IS STORED

» **RESOLUTION:** ALAN MANAGES TO KEEP THE MINE IN ORBIT WITH HIS ACROBATIC PILOTING UNTIL THE RIGHT DEACTIVATION CODE IS FOUND AND EVENTUALLY THE MINE IS DISARMED

» **LEARNINGS:** NEVER TAKE A JOB FOR GRANTED

VIRGIL TRACY

» **CRAFT:** THUNDERBIRD 2
» **TASK:** DEMOLITION, HEAVY LIFTING AND LOGISTICS
» **LIKELY TO SAY:** "TIME FOR SOME HEAVY LIFTING"

THUNDERBIRD 2

THUNDERBIRD 2

•• INTERNATIONAL RESCUE ••

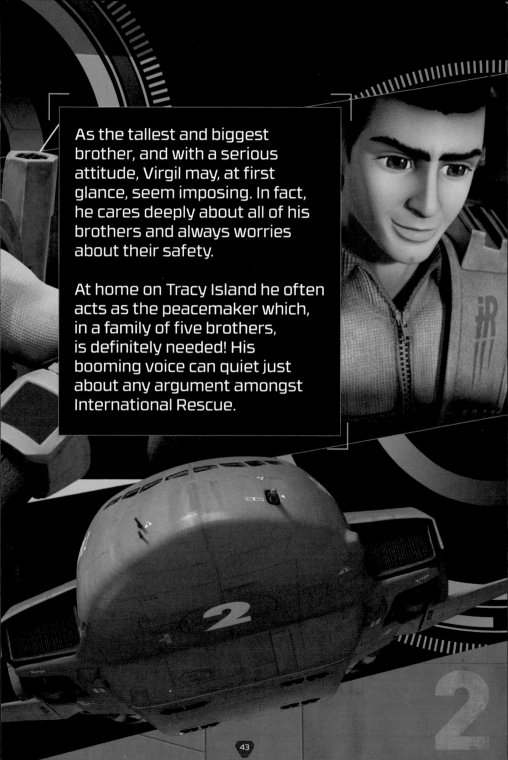

As the tallest and biggest brother, and with a serious attitude, Virgil may, at first glance, seem imposing. In fact, he cares deeply about all of his brothers and always worries about their safety.

At home on Tracy Island he often acts as the peacemaker which, in a family of five brothers, is definitely needed! His booming voice can quiet just about any argument amongst International Rescue.

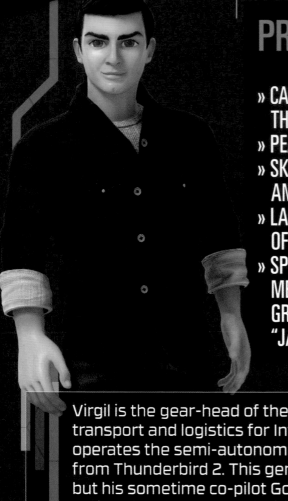

PROFILE:

- » CALM, LEVEL-HEADED AND THOROUGH
- » PEACEMAKER IN THE FAMILY
- » SKILLED IN ENGINEERING AND MECHANICS
- » LARGEST AND STRONGEST OF THE BROTHERS
- » SPECIALISED EQUIPMENT: MECHANICALLY ASSISTED GRASPING ARMS (AKA "JAWS OF LIFE")

Virgil is the gear-head of the group and is in charge of transport and logistics for International Rescue. He operates the semi-autonomous rescue equipment from Thunderbird 2. This gentle giant prefers peace but his sometime co-pilot Gordon keeps his more serious brother amused with his jokes and wisecracks!

Virgil is always there if special equipment is needed. TB2 is fully equipped with everything he needs so he is ready for any situation that may arise. His brothers can always rely on him to have the right tool for the job.

GADGETS:

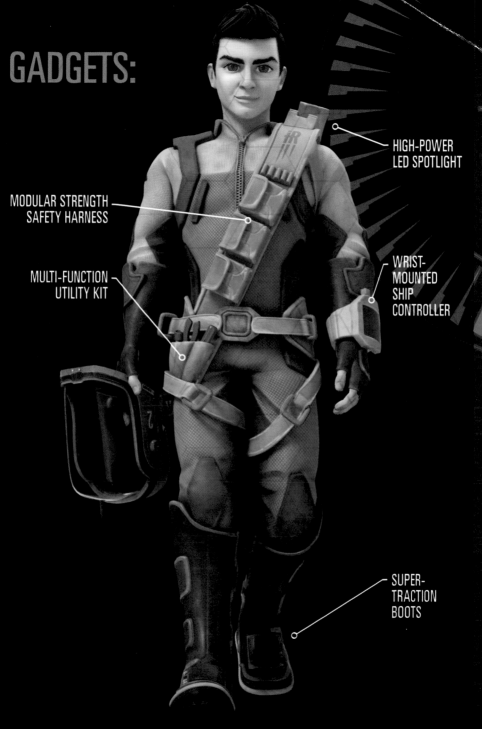

HIGH-POWER
LED SPOTLIGHT

MODULAR STRENGTH
SAFETY HARNESS

MULTI-FUNCTION
UTILITY KIT

WRIST-
MOUNTED
SHIP
CONTROLLER

SUPER-
TRACTION
BOOTS

THUNDERBIRD 2

» FUNCTION: AUXILIARY EQUIPMENT TRANSPORT
» TOP SPEED: 5000 MPH
» MAX ALTITUDE: 100,000 FEET
» PAYLOAD: UP TO 100 TONS
» EQUIPMENT: CAHELIUM SUPPORT FRAME, ONBOARD P.O.D. ASSEMBLY
FACTORY, ELECTROMAGNETIC CABLE LAUNCHER. THE CENTRE SECTION CAN
SEPARATE FROM THE OUTER SHELL ALLOWING TB2 TO PARTICIPATE IN
RESCUES IN A DIFFERENT LOCATION FROM WHERE THE PODS
ARE BEING DEPLOYED.

HIGH SPEED
MANOEUVRE
FLAPS

PRIMARY THRUST NOZZLES

VTOL
THRUSTER

CAN STAY ALOFT FOR AN ALMOST INDEFINITE PERIOD
OF TIME – THERE ARE EVEN FULL LIVING QUARTERS
ON BOARD IF NEEDED. CAN LAND ALMOST ANYWHERE.

THUNDERBIRD 2

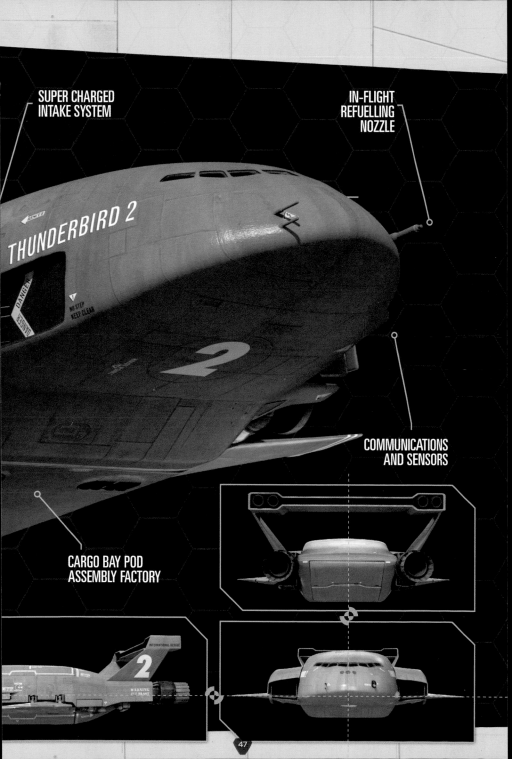

SUPER CHARGED
INTAKE SYSTEM

IN-FLIGHT
REFUELLING
NOZZLE

THUNDERBIRD 2

COMMUNICATIONS
AND SENSORS

CARGO BAY POD
ASSEMBLY FACTORY

VIRGIL TRACY
// KEY MISSION REPORT:
UNPLUGGED

» **LOCATION:** LONDON

» **OBJECTIVE:** AN ANTI-TECHNOLOGY GROUP,
THE LUDDITES, HAVE SET OFF AN ELECTRO-
MAGNETIC PULSE DEVICE CRIPPLING ANYTHING
THAT USES ELECTRICITY

» **CRISIS:** VIRGIL HAS NO WAY OF ACCESSING HIS
BROTHERS OR USING ANY OF THUNDERBIRD 2'S
RESOURCES SO HE AND GRANDMA TRACY MUST
WORK TOGETHER TO RESTORE POWER TO LONDON

» **BREAKTHROUGH:** LADY PENELOPE AND PARKER
DISCOVER THAT THE HOOD IS BEHIND THE LUDDITES'
ACTIONS, SO HE CAN BREAK INTO A VAULT AND
STEAL A UNIVERSAL GRID CODEX

» **RESOLUTION:** VIRGIL STOPS THE EMP DEVICE
AND RESTORES POWER. THE HOOD ESCAPES
BUT WITHOUT THE CODEX

» **LEARNING:** SOMETIMES THE SIMPLEST SOLUTION
CAN BE THE BEST

GLOBAL DEFENCE FORCE

On 2060 Earth there is a World Council made up of representatives of all countries. They are the main governing body on the planet and work together to make sure resources are not unfairly divided and ensure technological advancement for all. However, there are those in society who do not agree with this and are not satisfied with the current rate of progress. They want more and they want it all for themselves. They're willing to pollute, destroy and sacrifice the safety of others to achieve what they want. This means there is still a need for a security force, and this task of defending against villainy and bringing bad guys to justice falls on the shoulders of the Global Defence Force.

The GDF's soliders answer to the World Council but are independent of any sovereign nation meaning they can remain unbiased in any situation. They have outposts all over the globe, but rely on technology and efficiency to keep their ranks small.

GDF JET

TB5 IN GEOSTATIONARY ORBIT

The World Council would like to control International Rescue but the Tracys won't allow it. They wish to remain as independent as possible but, despite this, will work alongside the GDF. International Rescue often thwart the efforts of evil-doers during their rescue operations, but they won't specifically go after bad guys. The GDF does, leaving International Rescue to deal with the aftermath . . .

SCOTT TRACY

» **CRAFT:** THUNDERBIRD 1
» **TASK:** FIRST RESPONDER
» **LIKELY
  TO SAY:** "WE CAN HANDLE IT"

INTERNATIONA

In theory, International Rescue works as a team with no recognised leader, but in reality Scott steps into this role. As the oldest brother he has been a part of International Rescue for the longest time. He is intensely focussed on doing a good job and for him, the rescue business is serious business. He is bold and won't hesitate to jump into any situation. His instincts are often right but the few times they aren't Scott will agonise over any missed opportunity or mistake.

PROFILE:

» TEAM LEADER
» BOLD AND DECISIVE DECISION MAKER
» FEARLESS IN ACTION
» OLDEST AND MOST EXPERIENCED
» SPECIALISED EQUIPMENT: JETPACK, GRAPPLE LAUNCHER

Scott's leadership and manner can sometimes cause friction amongst the team, in other words, he can be a little bossy! But as the first responder he needs to be assertive, as it's his decisions that direct the rescue. He is bold at all times, never hesitating to jump out of a plane or dive into a lava-filled chasm for the good of the rescue.

His brothers respect his bold, fearless attitude and understand that at the heart of all his decisions is the success of International Rescue.

GADGETS:

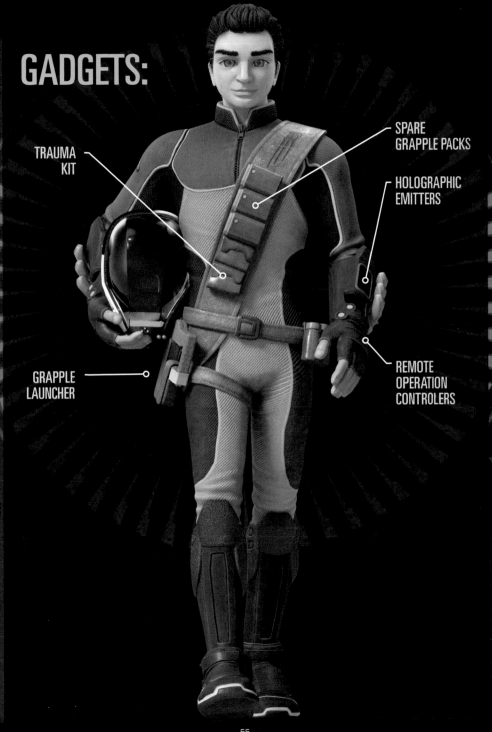

SPARE
GRAPPLE PACKS

HOLOGRAPHIC
EMITTERS

TRAUMA
KIT

REMOTE
OPERATION
CONTROLERS

GRAPPLE
LAUNCHER

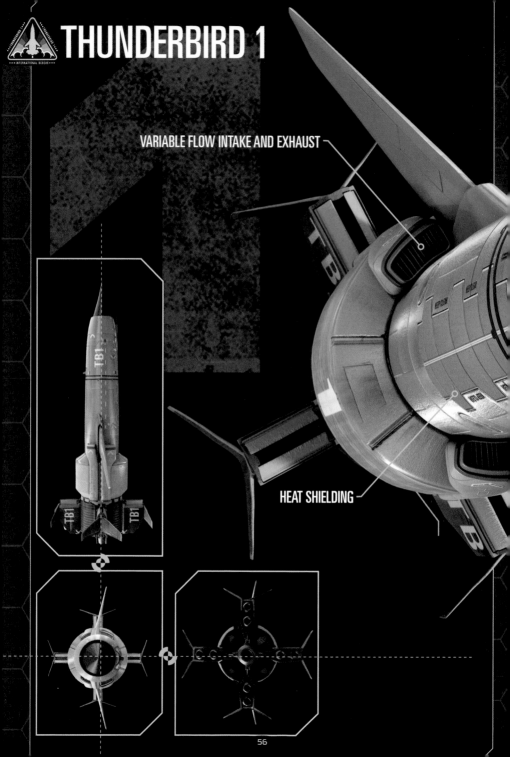

THUNDERBIRD 1

VARIABLE FLOW INTAKE AND EXHAUST

HEAT SHIELDING

COCKPIT

AVIONICS

VTOL HATCH

» FUNCTION: FAST RESPONSE CRAFT
» TOP SPEED: 15,000 MPH
» MAX ALTITUDE: 150,000 FEET
» EQUIPMENT:
SONAR, RADAR, VISUAL SPECTRUM, ULTRAVIOLET, ELECTROMAGNETIC
FIELD BUFFERS, ISOTOPIC SHIELDING, M.I.D.A.S. ANTI-DETECTION
SYSTEM. CAN REACH ANYWHERE ON THE PLANET IN 30 MINUTES OR
LESS. CANNOT CARRY MUCH AUXILIARY EQUIPMENT BUT DOES HAVE
A VARIETY OF RESCUE DEVICES ON BOARD. CAN BE REMOTE PILOTED IF
NEEDED USING AUTO-PILOT. HAS A VARIETY OF DESTRUCTIVE DEVICES
SO CAN BREAK THROUGH ROCK AND RUBBLE, CLEAR VEGETATION AND
CUT THROUGH METAL. CAPABLE OF VERTICAL TAKE OFF AND LANDING.
STABILISING THRUSTERS ALSO MEAN IT CAN HOVER.

SCOTT TRACY
// KEY MISSION REPORT:
CROSSCUT

» **LOCATION:** AN ABANDONED
   URANIUM MINE

» **OBJECTIVE:** TO STOP A RADIATION
   LEAK FROM THE MINE

» **CRISIS:** THERE'S A HUGE RADIATION
   LEAK THREATENING TO SPREAD ACROSS SOUTHERN
   AFRICA. SCOTT MUST SHUT DOWN THE LEAK, FIND
   A WAY OUT AND CONVINCE THE MINE OWNER'S
   DAUGHTER TO NOT SELL ANY OF THE DANGEROUS
   URANIUM TO THE HOOD

» **BREAKTHROUGH:** USING THE REMOTE PILOT ACTION ON
   THUNDERBIRD 1 TO LOWER A CABLE DOWN
   AS AN ESCAPE ROUTE

» **RESOLUTION:** VIRGIL ENDS UP SAVING HIS BROTHER
   USING THE MOLE POD TO CATCH THEM AFTER TB1'S
   CABLE SNAPS IN HIGH WINDS

» **LEARNING:** FIRST IMPRESSIONS ARE NOT ALWAYS THE
   WHOLE STORY

THE HOOD

In a world that is built upon science and engineering, technology is like currency. Those who have it can influence and control global situations. These people are extremely dangerous. They work in the shadows to gain power. The most ruthless, greedy and dangerous of all is The Hood. A true master of disguise, everything about this villain is an illusion. International Rescue and the Global Defence Force named him 'The Hood' because of his ability to change himself so totally and hide in plain sight. He has many alter-egos, each providing him with the cover and credibility he needs to act out his evil plans.

His masquerades are so complete they almost seem like magic. He is completely unrecognisable when disguised. To achieve these complete transformations he uses a futuristic holographic array and nanoscopic light emitters in his clothing, which together allow him to change his appearance in the blink of an eye.

THE HOOD V KAYO

THE HOOD & HENCHMEN

His life's mission is to steal and exploit cutting-edge technology. The more technology he can control, the more powerful he will be. Of course, no group on Earth has more advanced technology than International Rescue, and for this reason they are his number one target.

KAYO

» **CRAFT:** THUNDERBIRD S
» **TASK:** COVERT OPS
» **LIKELY TO SAY:** "SPOILING YOUR PLAN IS THE BEST PART OF MY JOB"

THUNDERBIRD THUNDERBIRD

INTERNATIONAL RESCUE

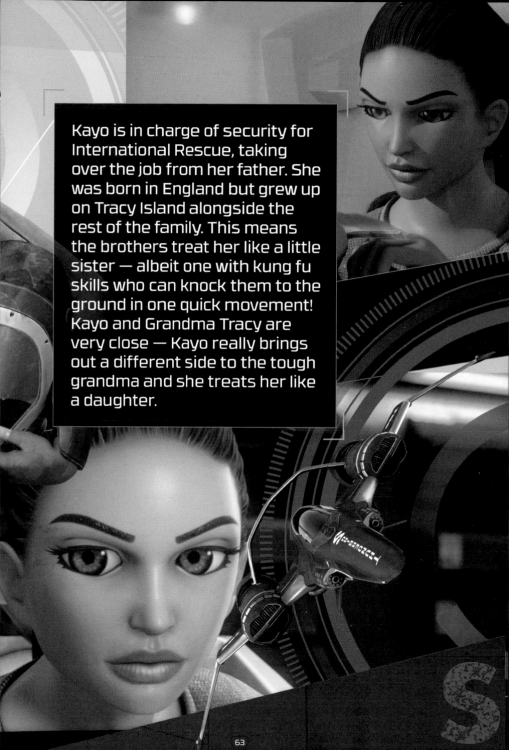

Kayo is in charge of security for International Rescue, taking over the job from her father. She was born in England but grew up on Tracy Island alongside the rest of the family. This means the brothers treat her like a little sister — albeit one with kung fu skills who can knock them to the ground in one quick movement! Kayo and Grandma Tracy are very close — Kayo really brings out a different side to the tough grandma and she treats her like a daughter.

PROFILE:

» **FULL NAME: TANUSHA "KAYO" KRYANO**
» **KUNG FU EXPERT**
» **HANDLES STEALTH MISSIONS**
» **QUIET AND EVER WATCHFUL**
» **TREATED LIKE FAMILY ON TRACY ISLAND**

As well as having a variety of acrobatic skills, Kayo is an expert in the Wing Chun form of kung fu. This all combines to make her a force to be reckoned with in any potential defensive combat situation. She trains the brothers in self defence, meaning they are ready for any dangerous situation they might find themselves in.

Her nickname came about as she was constantly (and accidentally) knocking out her sparring partners when she was younger — K.O. quickly turned into Kayo.

GADGETS:

DUAL HI-RES CAMERA AND HOLOGRAPHIC PROJECTOR

FULLY PRESSURIZED HIGH-ALTITUDE FLIGHT SUIT

PORTABLE ELECTRONICS JAMMER

CARBON NANO-FIBRE BODY ARMOUR

ADAPTABLE HARNESS WITH RAPPELLING PACK

STEALTH INTAKE

COCKPIT &
STOWAWAY
MOTORBIKE

MULTI-PURPOSE
LAUNCHER

THUNDERBIRD S

WING STABILISER

AFTER BURNER EXTENSION

POSTURAL
CONTROL
NOZZLE

» FUNCTION:
   STEALTH JET FOR TOP-SECRET MISSIONS
» EQUIPMENT:
   GRAPPLING CLAWS, HOLOGRAPHIC EMITTERS, SENSOR-
   DEFEATING ELECTRONICS, VTOL CAPABILITY SINGLE SEAT JET.
   COCKPIT SECTION CAN DETACH AND BE USED AS A MOTORBIKE.
   WINGS CAN FOLD UP IF LANDING SPACE IS TIGHT. GRAPPLING
   CLAWS ALLOW IT TO ATTACH TO VERTICAL SURFACES.
   PRACTICALLY UNDETECTABLE.

FIREFLASH

» LOCATION:
FLIGHT PATH TO AUSTRALIA

» OBJECTIVE: TO LAND A NEW SUPERSONIC PLANE
AFTER THE HOOD HAS SABOTAGED IT

» CRISIS: KAYO IS ON BOARD A FLIGHT TO AUSTRALIA WHEN
IT IS HIJACKED BY THE HOOD. HE ESCAPES BUT DAMAGES
THE PLANE'S LANDING GEAR. KAYO MUST LAND IT SAFELY
IN THE DESERT

» BREAKTHROUGH: VIRGIL, SCOTT, ALAN AND GORDON
WORK TOGETHER TO CREATE A MAKESHIFT LANDING
PLATFORM USING THUNDERBIRD 2'S PODS

» RESOLUTION: KAYO LANDS THE PLANE SAFELY

» LEARNING:
IT'S ALWAYS BEST TO STAY CALM IN DIFFICULT SITUATIONS

BRANS

» **ROLE:** ENGINEER
» **TASK:** DESIGNS AND BUILDS
VEHICLES AND TECHNOLOGY
» **TRAITS:** BRILLIANT,
CONTEMPLATIVE,
AND DELIBERATE
DOES NOT WORK
WELL UNDER
PRESSURE
» **LIKELY** "NOTHING'S IMPOSSIBLE
TO SAY: WITH SCIENCE!"

MAX

MAX

INTERNATIONAL RESCUE

M.A.X.

» **ROLE:** MECHANICAL ASSISTANT (EXPERIMENTAL)
» **TASK:** ROBOT HELPER TEST SUBJECT FOR BRAINS' INVENTIONS
» **TRAITS:** ONLY BRAINS CAN UNDERSTAND HIM

COMMUNICATIONS ARRAY

OPTICAL AND THERMAL SCANNER

AUTONOMOUS POWER AND CONTROL MODULE

ADAPTABLE ALL-TERRAIN MOBILITY LIMBS

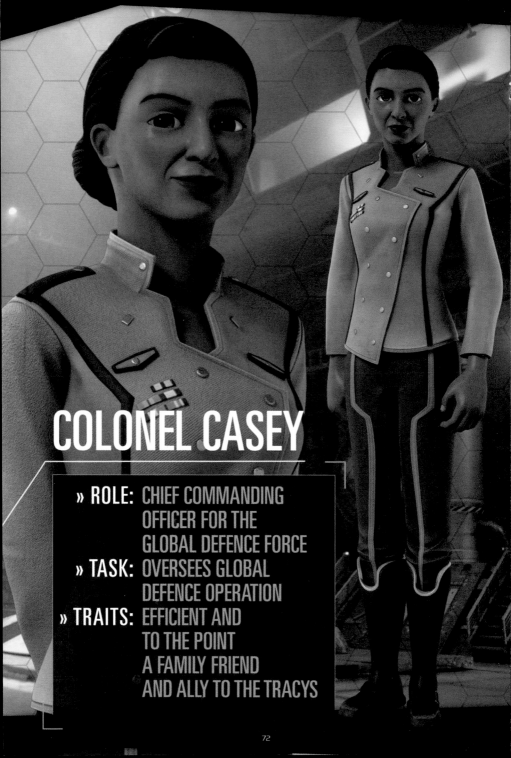

COLONEL CASEY

» **ROLE:** CHIEF COMMANDING
OFFICER FOR THE
GLOBAL DEFENCE FORCE
» **TASK:** OVERSEES GLOBAL
DEFENCE OPERATION
» **TRAITS:** EFFICIENT AND
TO THE POINT
A FAMILY FRIEND
AND ALLY TO THE TRACYS

GRANDMA

» **ROLE:** MANAGES TRACY ISLAND
» **TRAITS:** TERRIBLE COOK
FULL OF WISDOM
AND INSIGHT
HAS AN OPINION ON
JUST ABOUT ANYTHING
» **LIKELY
TO SAY:** "WHERE THERE'S TIME
TO LEAN, THERE'S TIME
TO CLEAN!"

LADY PENELOPE

- » **ROLE:** LONDON AGENT
- » **TASK:** BEHIND THE SCENES 'FIXER' FOR INTERNATIONAL RESCUE
- » **TRAITS:** FAMOUS INFLUENTIAL SOCIALITE
  A SMOOTH OPERATOR WITH A DRY WIT AND A GREAT SENSE OF PURPOSE
- » **LIKELY TO SAY:** "THIS IS RATHER DISTRESSING"

SHERBERT

- » **ROLE:** LADY PENELOPE'S FAMOUS TRAVEL COMPANION
- » **TRAITS:** SENSES WHEN THERE IS TROUBLE OR DECEPTION
  DOES NOT GET ALONG WITH PARKER

PARKER

- » **ROLE:** BODYGUARD AND DRIVER FORMER SOLDIER WITH DECORATED SERVICE RECORD
- » **TRAITS:** SHADY PAST HELPS HIM UNDERSTAND CRIMINALS DROLL, UNFLAPPABLE COCKNEY CHAP REFERS TO LADY PENELOPE AS M'LADY
- » **LIKELY TO SAY:** "M'LADY"

FAB 1

LADY PENELOPE TRAVELS IN A SLEEK, STATE OF THE ART, SIX-WHEELED, CHAUFFEUR DRIVEN LIMOUSINE. FROM THE VAST ARRAY OF COMMUNICATIONS EQUIPMENT TO PUNCTURE PROOF TYRES AND A BULLETPROOF BODY, FAB 1 IS MORE THAN JUST A STYLISH CAR.

INDEX